MY SINGING monsters

MUSIC ISLAND MISSIONS

ZOSHLING ENCOUNTERS

PUFFIN BOOKS

Published by the Penguin Group
Penguin Books Ltd, 80 Strand, London WC2R 0RL, England
Penguin Group (USA) Inc., 375 Hudson Street, New York, New York 10014,
USA Penguin Group (Canada), 90 Eglinton Avenue East, Suite 700,
Toronto, Ontario, Canada M4P 2Y3 (a division of Pearson Penguin Canada Inc.)
Penguin Ireland, 25 St Stephen's Green, Dublin 2, Ireland
a division of Penguin Books Ltd)
Penguin Group (Australia), 707 Collins Street, Melbourne, Victoria 3008,
Australia (a division of Pearson Australia Group Pty Ltd)
Penguin Books India Pvt Ltd, 11 Community Centre, Panchsheel Park,
New Delhi – 110 017, India
Penguin Group (NZ), 67 Apollo Drive, Rosedale, Auckland 0632,
New Zealand (a division of Pearson New Zealand Ltd)
Penguin Books (South Africa) (Pty) Ltd, Block D, Rosebank Office Park,
181 Jan Smuts Avenue, Parktown North, Gauteng 2193, South Africa

Penguin Books Ltd, Registered Offices: 80 Strand, London WC2R 0RL, England

puffinbooks.com

First published 2013
001

Written by Sue Behrent
Illustrations by Abigail Ryder

Text and illustrations copyright © Mind Candy Ltd, 2013
Moshi Monsters is a trademark of Mind Candy Ltd. All rights reserved

The moral right of the author and illustrator has been asserted

Set in Adobe Garamond Pro
Printed in Great Britain by Clays Ltd, St Ives plc

British Library Cataloguing in Publication Data
A CIP catalogue record for this book is available from the British Library

ISBN: 978-1-409-39221-7

ALWAYS LEARNING

PEARSON

ZOSHLING ENCOUNTERS

T SHREWMAN

PUFFIN

CONTENTS

Chapter 1

SUPER MOSHI TRAINING TIME

In a clearing in the forest that bordered Monstro City the sounds of splintering wood, splattering goo-balls and combat kicks filled the air.

CRRRRRRRR-ACK! GOOP-SPLAAAAAT!! "Hiiiiii-YAH!"

The Super Moshis were in full training mode!

Their mission: to defeat the evil crime syndicate, C.L.O.N.C. (the Criminal League of Naughty Critters), which had launched an attack on Monstro City and was responsible for the mysterious disappearance of the Super Moshis' beloved leader, Elder Furi.

SPLAT!!

'ZOMMER! Watch what you're goo-ing!' Katsuma yelled as he wiped a slimy mess off the back of his neck.

'Sorry, Katsuma.' Zommer grinned sheepishly as he lurched over to his friend. 'I was just practising flicking these goo-balls. Elder Furi said if I want to improve my skills I have to keep trying.'

'Well, be careful where you're aiming, eh?' Katsuma huffed.

Zommer scratched his head as he thought this over, accidentally unpicking a stitch or two from the seam that ran across his forehead. Although he was a faithful friend dedicated to helping those in need, Zommer's thirst for wobbleade had left him a few zombies short of a full-blown invasion. 'Yeah, OK,' he replied slowly. 'I'll be careful.'

Katsuma sighed.

'I'm sorry for being such a grump, Zom,' he said, picking up a plank from the ground and laying it across the top of two logs. 'I'm just really worried about Elder Furi. It makes me so angry to think of him in the hands of Dr. Strangeglove and his hideous C.L.O.N.C. henchmen. I promise you, when we find them, I'll – Hiiiiii-YAH!'

Katsuma raised his paw and sliced cleanly through the piece of wood in front of him.

'Very impressive!' Luvli cried from the treetops, where she was practising dusting her Shimmering Sparkle Shower. 'Your paws are deadly weapons, Katsuma!'

'They'll be more use in our next battle against Strangeglove than that glitter you're always chucking about,' he laughed.

'As I've told you a zillion times before, Katsuma,' said Luvli, a frown creasing her heart-shaped face, 'my Sparkle Shower is a more subtle weapon. It fools my enemies and creates a diversion –'

Katsuma ignored her, bending down to set up another plank.

'– allowing me to strike!' Luvli unfurled her

star-tipped stem, striking the plank Katsuma was holding with a KISHHHHHH!

'WHOA!' Katsuma leapt back in shock. He stared in astonishment at the piece of wood he'd dropped – smoke curled up from the star-shaped hole burnt right through it!

'She got you there,' laughed Poppet as she and Furi broke off their Kung Fu practice to join Katsuma and Zommer.

'I've got to admit, Luvli, that was very cool!' Katsuma laughed. 'Maybe I have misjudged your sparkle powder.'

'Sparkle Shower,' Luvli corrected him, rolling her eyes.

'I like that trick, Luvli. And yours too, Katsuma,' grinned Furi, picking up the smoking plank. 'But can either of you do this?'

'Wait, Furi, stop . . . !' Diavlo yelled, darting over to his friend, but it was too late.

THWACK! Furi brought the plank down as hard as he could on his furry head, spraying his friends with splinters. He looked around and smiled proudly.

'I'm clever, aren't I, Diavlo? Eh? I could beat that C.L.O.N.C. crook Strangeglove in a fight any day, eh, Diavlo?' He turned to the fire-starting buddy hovering beside him, then frowned. 'Hey, why are there so many Diavlos flying in circles round my head? Stop that, Diavlos, you're making me feel sick!'

The rest of the Super Moshis looked wearily at each other and stepped out of the way as Furi swatted the empty air around him. Once again, he'd smacked himself in the head just a little too hard.

Across town, inside the Observatory at The Port, Monstro City's resident scientific genius was waiting for the printouts of her latest deep-space scans. But just as she sat down to study the numbers a loud, wailing alarm made her jump.

WOOOOOH! WOOOOOH!

It was her searchometer! That alarm meant only one thing: an unidentified flying object had entered Monstro City!

The Super Moshis' training was over for the day. They lay exhausted under a tree, surrounded by smashed-up pieces of wood, dirty glitter and drying goo-balls.

'I wish the Gatekeeper would let us into Elder Furi's mission-control room,' sighed Poppet, idly picking at the grass. 'There must be a clue in there somewhere that'd help us find him.'

'Without Elder Furi's permission? Forget it!' said Katsuma. 'The Gatekeeper's pretty suspicious! He always thinks we're up to something.'

'We usually are!' Diavlo said. 'Remember that time

we tricked him by dressing up like a lady Gatekeeper and getting him to take us to the movies?'

The Super Moshis all burst out laughing. They'd played loads of tricks on the Gatekeeper – all in the name of fun, of course!

'It's a complete waste of time appealing to that block of wood for help,' said Zommer.

'Yep. There's no point axing him to do us any

favours,' grinned Poppet.

'The Gatekeeper's never been able to hack our practical jokes,' snickered Luvli.

'He always fell for them though,' chortled Furi. 'But, seriously, we should cut it out.'

The Super Moshis laughed so hard at their silly jokes that tears poured down their cheeks and their tummies hurt! They were still giggling when Diavlo's Mini Moshifone started ringing.

Are you ready for the show? Shake your body to and fro.

'Diavlo's ringtone is the "The Missy Kix Dance"?' giggled Zommer, as Diavlo answered the phone. 'I've always seen him as more of a Squeezy Tinklehuff fan.'

'Same! Or a Jolly Tubthu . . .' Katsuma suddenly trailed off as he noticed how pale Diavlo had become. Well, as pale as someone with a head full of lava *can* turn.

Covering the mouthpiece with his hand, Diavlo looked around at his crime-fighting friends.

'It's Tamara Tesla. She needs to see us right away!'

Chapter 2

ONE HOT MISSION!

'I'll get straight to the point, Super Moshis,' said Tamara Tesla as the monsters crowded into the Observatory. 'My searchometer has picked up an unidentified flying object that appears to have crash-landed in the jungle on Music Island.'

The Supers immediately started murmuring with excitement.

'I understand you want to find Elder Furi,' continued Tamara, raising her voice above the hubbub. 'But under the circumstances I think this is worth checking out first.'

'Absolutely!' cried Poppet. 'If someone's in trouble, we need to help them. Plus, a visit to Music Island would be cool – it's home to some of the hottest gooperstars around!'

'We'll need transportation to get there,' said Furi.

'Right! And who do we know who has a private Sneerjet and owes us big time?' said Katsuma. 'Simon Growl!'

'You should call him, Luvli, and use the ol' Glittery Charm Offensive,' said Zommer.

Luvli winked cheekily and dialled the pop manager's mobile number.

Across town on Music Island, Simon Growl scowled and hung up his Mini Moshifone.

'GAH! I don't know how or why,' he muttered to himself, 'but I've agreed to help the Super Moshis.'

Simon's hair growled moodily as he hurried into his mansion. He'd better have time to iron his high-waisted trousers.

A few minutes later, the Super Moshis tumbled into Growl's private scareport. They were super-excited about meeting the celebrities on Music Island!

'I want Missy Kix's autograph,' said Furi.

'Me too! And Zack Binspin's!' laughed Poppet. 'Oh, and Moptop Tweenybop is my all-time favourite! Hey, what's going on over there?'

Poppet pointed at a large crowd of Moshis. Some of them were holding homemade signs. 'Moshling Mania!' said one. 'Binspin makes my head spin!' said another.

The Supers watched as the crowd began to surge and excited squeals filled the scareport.

'I'll do a flyover and find out what's happening!' Luvli shouted above the noise.

She circled above the excited monsters, then signalled for the Supers to follow her to a quiet corner. The only person around was a cleaner mopping the floor.

'It's Zack Binspin!' Luvli explained. 'He's being mobbed by fans and scareport security can't get him to his plane.'

The monsters thought for a moment, then Katsuma raised a paw. 'I've got an idea.' He nodded over to the cleaner and called, 'Excuse me, Mr Cleaning Guy? A quick word?'

'Sure, Super Moshis,' said the cleaner, propping his mop against a vending machine and coming over to join them.

'Bring the mop, dude. You'll need it,' said Katsuma, and turned to the Supers to explain his plan.

Five minutes later the crowd surrounding Zack Binspin had swelled to twice its original size. Their screaming was deafening.

'This had better work, Katsuma,' shouted Luvli.

'It will,' Katsuma promised with a wink. 'Let's go over it one more time. You fly ahead and drop the cleaner's uniform to Binspin while we distract the crowd. When the fans are looking at us, they'll see the cleaner – except he'll be wearing his regular clothes and the mop as a wig. The fans will think it's Zack! When the fake makes a sprint for the exit, they'll follow him right out of the scareport, leaving the real Binspin free to board his plane!'

The Moshis took a deep breath and put Katsuma's idea into action. Luvli needn't have worried; it unfolded exactly as planned – plus one final masterstroke. To

avoid any further trouble, Katsuma hid Zack Binspin in a rubbish bin and rolled him out to the runway! Although being from Brashcan Alley, Zack didn't mind one bit.

Simon Growl tapped his watch meaningfully as the Super Moshis appeared on the runway, rolling a rubbish bin.

'I've been waiting for aaaaages!' he drawled irritably,

hitching his trousers up even higher.

'Sorry! We had to help Zack Binspin escape some crazed fans,' explained Furi, yanking the bin lid and tipping out the woozy singer.

Growl ignored the Moshling gooperstar.

'Well, I've got a much bigger problem. It appears that Hairosniff "borrowed" the Sneerjet and made a complete mess of it.' He pointed over at the tatty Sneerjet parked behind the Supers. Broken bits of plane lay scattered on the ground and the wings were dotted with graffiti. 'Very rock and roll I'm sure! But we won't be going anywhere until you fix it.'

'But we don't know –' began Zommer, before Growl cut him off.

'But? But? Just fix it!' he ordered, and with a final snarl of his hair Simon Growl flounced off to the First Class Lounge, snapping his fingers at Binspin to follow.

'Thanks for saving me, Super Moshis,' purred Zack as he trailed after Growl. 'Laterz!'

As Binspin disappeared, the Supers turned back to study the broken Sneerjet.

'It's going to take forever to get this heap of junk up and running,' said Zommer.

'You can say that again,' sighed Luvli.

'It's going to take –'

'Not now, Zom,' snapped Diavlo.

The Super Moshis were wondering where to start when a small creature fluttered over to them.

'Hey, guys, was that Simon Growl and Zack Binspin I just saw?' it asked hopefully.

'Sure was,' Furi replied. 'Who wants to know?'

'I'm Gurgle the Performing Flappasaurus and I've been trying desperately to get an appointment to see Mr Growl,' it explained.

Zommer peered at the Moshling dino.

'Hey, I've seen your act!' he exclaimed. 'You pulled a Potty Pipsqueak out of a hat and afterwards –'

'Yes, that would've been me. I'm a magician. Tricks an' that,' burbled Gurgle nervously.

'Yeah, someone heckled you and you got really upset!' Zommer continued.

'Did I? Well, I don't remember every –'

'You burst into tears and accidentally breathed fire at the same time and all your props burnt to a crisp!' Zommer finished triumphantly.

Gurgle's wings drooped miserably.

'Yeah, sounds like me,' he sighed. 'Now I'm working here at the scareport on the maintenance crew. I'm trying to save Rox so I can buy more props. I'd give anything to audition for Simon Growl!'

'You should; it was an amazing act!' Zommer assured him.

'Soooo, you belong to the maintenance crew and you fix planes . . . like this one behind us, right?' Poppet asked coyly.

Gurgle nodded.

'Well,' Poppet grinned, 'if you and your guys repair this Sneerjet, we'll make sure you get the chance to perform your act for Simon Growl!'

'Awesome!' Gurgle whooped. 'I'll call the crew!'

The Super Moshis smiled. At last, something was going right.

The maintenance crew had the Sneerjet ready to go in less than an hour. Even Simon Growl had been impressed – well, sort of.

Now they were airborne and on their way to Music

Island with Gurgle smuggled aboard.

With half an hour of the flight remaining, Poppet picked up the intercom.

'To thank Mr Growl and Mr Binspin for allowing

us to hitch a ride on this wonderful Sneerjet, we've organized a little in-flight entertainment . . .'

'WHAT?' Growl's roar came booming out of the luxury lounge at the front of the Sneerjet.

'I sure hope Gurgle nails this,' said Katsuma as the act's intro music wafted down the aisle to Economy. 'I hate to think what would happen if Simon Growl criticized him.'

'Growl's gonna go nuts,' said Zommer. 'Gurgle's magic show is terrible!'

'*What?* Earlier you said it was awesome!' Katsuma cried.

'I had to say something!' said Zommer defensively. 'Didn't you see the little dude's face when I mentioned the whole props-fire thing? He was heartbroken!'

'Fire?' Luvli looked at Katsuma.

'On a plane?' Katsuma looked at Poppet.

'AIIIIIIIIIIIIIIEEEEEEE!'

Right on cue, the smell of scorched seating filled the jet.

Chapter 3

BUSTER'S MOSHLING QUEST

The Sneerjet had barely touched down on Music Island before its doors flew open. Black smoke billowed out, followed by the sound of coughing and spluttering. The smoke cleared slowly to reveal Simon Growl in the doorway, his face purple with rage. His hair didn't look too happy, either.

'**GET. OFF. MY. PLANE!**' he bellowed between gasps of fresh air.

One by one the Super Moshis and Gurgle staggered off the plane, smoky tears streaming down their faces.

Zack Binspin stumbled out next, followed by Growl himself.

Everyone was covered with black soot and the distinct aroma of singed fringes and scorched fur hung in the air.

'I'll be sending you the cleaning bill, you Super Moshi morons!' Simon Growl spat, climbing into the scareport buggy sent to ferry him and Binspin to the arrivals hall.

'Ignore Simon – he's wigging out,' whispered Binspin as Growl's hair snapped and snarled at the Super Moshis. 'I thought the magic show was kind of a blast.'

'It certainly would've been had the flames reached the Sneerjet's fuel

tank,' muttered Luvli darkly.

'Come on, Zack!' Growl hollered.

With a final wink, Binspin jumped into the buggy and they sped off.

Poppet breathed out. 'Well, that show didn't go quite as planned.'

'Really? As far as I remember – what with the alarms, the screaming and the rapidly spreading flames – that's exactly how Gurgle's last show finished,' said Zommer, with a shrug. 'That fire-breathing finale sure is something, Gurgle! What did you think, Katsuma? Gurgle's really got a flare for magic, eh? Heh.'

'Please don't talk to me,' huffed Katsuma, striding towards the arrivals hall.

Ten minutes later, the Super Moshis had cleaned up and said goodbye to Gurgle, who was flying back to Monstro City under his own steam. Quite literally –

his fire-breathing antics had created a lot of it!

They were just about to leave the scareport when Diavlo spotted someone they knew.

'Hey, isn't that Buster Bumblechops?'

Diavlo pointed over to the luggage carousel, where Bumblechops, Monstro City's expert Moshling collector, was wrestling with his equipment.

'I think he needs our help . . .' said Furi as Buster loaded a stack of cages on to a scareport trolley, only to accidentally knock them off again with the long handle of a Moshling net.

The Super Moshis trotted over and began grabbing cages and nets, and neatly stacking them on trolleys.

'Oh, Super Moshis! Very kind,' smiled Buster with surprise.

'You sure have a lot of stuff, Buster,' Diavlo laughed.

'Quite a bit of kit needed when you're on a Moshling hunt, y'know,' said Buster, eyeing the four trolleys of luggage. 'Although I didn't think I'd

brought quite so much . . .'

He was right! In their haste to get Bumblechops organized, the Super Moshis had accidentally grabbed a bag that didn't belong to him. Buster's stuff was all old and battered, but this was a fancy leather suitcase with 'SG' printed all over it.

'I'm travelling into the Gombala Gombala Jungle in search of rare Nutties Moshlings for my collection,' Buster explained as the Supers gathered round. 'I have a four-squeal-drive car if you need a lift anywhere on the island . . . ?'

'That'd be great,' said Luvli enthusiastically. 'We're on a mission to find a UFO, and Tamara Tesla said it'd crashed in the jungle.'

'That's settled then,' smiled Buster, marching off towards the scareport exit, leaving the Supers to follow with his mountain of gear.

After they'd loaded the cases into the car, the Moshis jockeyed for space in the back.

'Move over!'

'No, you move over!'

'Urgh, yuck! I'm sitting on someone's snot-ball!'

In the driver's seat, Buster punched 'Gombala Gombala Jungle' into the GPS, the car's map system.

'What does GPS stand for?" asked Zommer.

'Gotta Point Somewhere!' said Buster Bumblechops, hitting the accelerator.

What they didn't notice was a dark figure hiding in the shadows, watching them as they sped away.

Katsuma sighed. He was pretty sure they'd just passed the same Dinky Dreamcloud-shaped rock for the fourth time.

'We're travelling in circles, Buster,' he moaned.

'We can't be!' Buster replied confidently. 'I'm using the GPS.'

Katsuma looked at Poppet and Luvli and mouthed, 'We're lost.'

Poppet grimaced and closed her eyes.

'Let's double check with a local anyway, eh, Buster?' suggested Luvli, fluttering her eyelashes at him.

'If you like,' Buster said, shrugging.

But there was no one around to ask. Since they'd left the scareport and turned inland away from the beach, they'd hardly seen anyone.

'According to Roary Scrawl lots of gooperstars live out here in the middle of nowhere,' said Furi. 'Away from prying fans and the Peppyrazzi!'

'I doubt you'll see any gooperstars,' said Buster. 'But keep your eyes peeled for Nutties. The jungle is their natural habitat and –'

'Look out!' Luvli yelled.

Something was walking right in the middle of the road!

Buster quickly yanked the steering wheel to the left. The car swerved up on to the grass at the side of the road and shuddered to a stop.

Buster looked out of the window at what he'd narrowly missed.

'I don't want to alarm anyone, but a large gold nugget with a boombox is approaching the car,' he said quietly.

The Super Moshis peered out.

'That's not a gold nugget,' said Diavlo. 'It's just someone wearing a gold necklace . . . and a gold

bracelet . . . and a gold ring . . . and, wow, that's a lot of gold!'

'It's . . . it's . . . oh my, it is! It's Blingo!' Furi said excitedly.

'WHAT?' Buster yelped. 'An ultra-rare Flashy Fox Moshling for my collection!'

Before the Supers could say a word, Buster jumped out of the driver's seat, grabbed a net and captured poor unsuspecting Blingo!

'Yo, man, what's the deal?' Blingo spluttered, his sunglasses askew. 'First you try to run me over and then you're up in my grill with this whole I-don't-even-know-what!' Blingo struggled against the netting.

'I'm catching you for my Moshling collection,' explained Buster.

'Look bro, get this veil off my head before I call my crew!' Blingo said huffily.

The Super Moshis had formed a semi-circle around Blingo and were staring at him, awestruck.

'Wow! I absolutely love 'Diggin' Ya Lingo', Blingo,' said Diavlo.

'Yeah, well how about you give grandpa here the downlow on how famous I am, and get me outta this thing!' Blingo snapped.

'Grandpa? Grandpa?!' Buster spluttered with rage. 'How dare – '

'You'll have to let Blingo go, Buster,' said Poppet gently. 'He's a gooperstar! Anyway, you're here to find Nutties, not Flashy Foxes.'

Buster looked from Poppet to Blingo and back to Poppet again and firmly shook his head.

'A Flashy Fox in the hand is worth two Nutties in the jungle,' he said decisively.

Chapter 4

WELCOME TO THE JUNGLE

'Whoa! Did someone say Nutties?' Blingo asked slyly. 'Cos I'm down with the Nutties.'

Buster was torn. He was desperate for a Flashy Fox Moshling, but if Blingo really was a gooperstar he wouldn't be able to keep him . . . and he did come to Music Island looking for Nutties . . .

Sighing loudly, Buster jerked the net off his captive's head.

'Where can I find them?' he snapped.

'Yo, if you've got a GPS in that heap o' junk there,' Blingo nodded towards the car, 'I've got the

coordinates for Nutties central – the Cacophony Caves! Though you'd better watch your step. Somethin' in the jungle is really fur-reeking those Nutties out!'

While Buster and Blingo programmed the Cacophony Caves into the GPS, the Supers formed a huddle.

'Did you hear what Blingo said?' Luvli asked. 'Something's making the Nutties even nuttier than usual. I think it might be the UFO.'

Suddenly they heard raised voices in the car . . .

'. . . it's broken! Can't you hear that hummin' sound?' Blingo was saying.

'B-but I just hired this car at the scareport,' Buster said hotly. 'And they assured me that –'

'And I assure you that this GPS is BUSTED!' Blingo shouted. 'That sucker is makin' the same tuneless squeaks my recordin' gear's been makin' lately.'

'Er, excuse me, Blingo?' Poppet broke in. 'Did you say there's something wrong with your studio equipment?'

'Yeah, I did! What do you think I'm doin' out

here listenin' to
my boombox?'
Blingo asked
grumpily. 'All my
electronics at home are
buzzin' – and not in a good
way. This is the only place I
can play my bangin' new tracks.
I'm on   ol'-skool battery power!'

Katsuma suddenly gasped and turned to the Supers.

'The crashed UFO must be sending out a distress
signal or something! That'd mess with all electronics
in the area.' He looked over his shoulder at Buster

and added, 'We really need to get a move on if we're going to find these Nutties, eh?'

Buster nodded.

'If you could just show me the Cacophony Caves on the fold-out map, Blingo?' he asked.

While Buster and Blingo studied the map of Music Island, the Super Moshis climbed back into the car. 'We're definitely closing in on the mystery spaceship,' said Luvli.

Buster soon joined them in the driver's seat and wound down his window.

'Thanks, Blingo,' he called cheerily. 'Sure we can't drop you anywhere?'

'Nuh-uh,' said Blingo with a half wave. 'The jungle's pretty fly – I'm quite enjoyin' myself. It's been a long time since I came down from the Hipsta Hills to become a gooperstar, so I'm gettin' back in touch with my roots. And all these tree roots too!'

The Super Moshis waved goodbye as Buster drove away, watching Blingo until they turned a curve and

he was lost from sight.

'Oh no!' Zommer cried, slapping his forehead. 'We forgot to get autographs!'

What the Super Moshis didn't see as they turned back to face the road was the scooter behind them. It had almost run over Blingo, who was so lost in his music that he didn't hear the tinny beep-beep of the horn until it was practically on top of him.

'Yo, wassup, dude, where's the party at?' he yelled angrily as he dived out of the way. 'Because those stripy strides are PARTY PANTS, man!'

Blingo shook his head as the scooter shot past. He couldn't remember the jungle ever being so busy before!

Buster's car turned on to a narrow lane and bumped along until it came to a large clearing where five beautiful Magical Mules were waiting. Buster had hired them to carry his Moshling-hunting equipment.

The Super Moshis tumbled out of the car and worked as a team, loading the mules up with the nets, cages, bags and other bits and bobs Buster had brought with him.

'Uh-oh,' said Poppet suddenly as she pulled a posh leather suitcase from the back of the car. 'Is this yours, Buster?'

'Nope, too fancy for me!' Buster laughed. 'Plus my initials aren't SG, like the letters all over this suitcase.'

'SG?' Katsuma exclaimed. 'We've accidentally grabbed someone else's stuff off the baggage carousel and I think it's Simon Growl's!'

The Super Moshis groaned. Yet another thing for him and his hair to get in a tizzy about!

'We'll give it back next time we see him,' said Luvli, tying the suitcase to a Magical Mule. 'He might've forgotten about the whole fire thing by then . . .'

The rest of the Supers eyed each other doubtfully.

Soon the Magical Mules were loaded up and the expedition was ready to head into the jungle.

'Now, remember, if you see any evidence of Nutties Moshlings, please let me know immediately,' urged Buster.

Several hours and many snack breaks later there was still no sign of Nutties Moshlings or UFO crash sites!

The Super Moshis were tired, dirty and covered in sillipede bites and, like all good expedition leaders, Buster Bumblechops sensed it was time to rally his troops.

'We're nearing the heart of the Gombala Gombala Jungle now, Super Moshis,' he said brightly. 'It won't be long until we reach Blingo's Cacophony Caves, where we'll be able to perform "The Summoning".'

'"The Summoning"? What's that?' Furi asked.

'It's an ancient poem handed down from one generation of Moshling collectors to the next,' replied Buster. 'It tells of how to capture CocoLoco, the Naughty Nutter. Would you like to hear it?'

'Yes, please!' the Supers cried. Ignoring the buzzing insects, they sprawled on the jungle floor and waited for Buster to begin.

Buster squatted down and after a moment began to chant in a quavering voice:

'To glimpse CocoLoco, the story tells,
You play a sweet tune on the Mungus Bells,
You might attract one, you might get a few,
But to entice them down, here's what you do . . .

To capture the Nutty, so wild and so free,
You will need the bass notes of the Saxoak Tree,
Played together with the drums of the Bongonium Flower
You'll soon have that Naughty Nutter deep in your power.

Added to these is the widdly Marimba,

Which must be played at a certain timbre.

The final ingredient is the talented frog choir;
When those guys get going, they're really on fire!
The thing to remember is you must persist
Cos music is something CocoLoco can't resist.'

'These instruments in the poem, they're all at the Cacophony Caves?' Poppet asked as she flicked a crawling caterpiggy off her leg.

'Yes, indeed,' replied Buster.

'And what about this frogestra, where do we find that?' Diavlo asked, swatting at a big, black fly that was buzzing annoyingly in front of his face.

Suddenly, Katsuma's lightning-fast paw zoomed in and caught it mid-buzz.

'Easy!' he grinned, holding up the bug for all to see. 'But we're gonna need a whole lot more of these.'

What the Super Moshis didn't see behind them was the gloved hand, reaching through the palm fronds and

snatching Simon Growl's suitcase from the back of a
Magic Mule.

WHEEEEEEEK!

As sneakily as it had appeared, the hand was gone . . .

Chapter 5

COCOLOCO AND CAPTAIN SQUIRK

By the time they reached Cacophony Caves, the adventurers had captured over a hundred insects.

'Quickly! Let's find the musical instruments!' Buster whooped excitedly. 'I'll point them out, Super Moshis, and you can have the honour of playing them!'

The Super Moshis stood by eagerly, awaiting Buster's orders.

'OK! I see Mungus Bells high in that tree,' hollered Bumblechops, pointing into the canopy. 'Fly up and ring them to get CocoLoco's attention!'

Diavlo flew up to the top of the tree and rang the fluorescent green bellflowers.

TING! TING! TING!

Everyone fell silent and waited.

All of a sudden they heard chittering from amongst the leaves, and CocoLoco's mischievous face appeared in the foliage.

'Next we need to blow the Saxoak Tree,' said Buster, pointing to a pink and purple trunk with a moss-covered growth in the shape of a big, brass instrument.

Katsuma trotted across and blew into the opening at the top of the trunk, producing a deep bass sound. MUUUUUUURK! MUUUUUUUUUURK! MUUUUUURK!

On a branch high above them CocoLoco nodded along to the music.

'It's working!' Buster hissed gleefully. 'Next the Marimba!' He waded through the undergrowth and stripped away some hanging vines, uncovering a long line of leaves poking out of a hole in a tree.

'Found them!' he cried, tapping them with his walking stick.

BLO-BLO-BLO!

CocoLoco leapt down to a lower branch to enjoy the music.

'One more instrument to go, my friends!' Buster said happily. 'The Bongonium Flowers! I see them, Luvli. Pink flowers with blue leaves, right above you!'

Luvli flew up and hovered over the tall Bongoniums, patting the blossoms.

PAH! PAH! PAH-PAH!

'We've done it!' Buster cried. But CocoLoco was still tantalizingly out of reach.

'Not quite, Buster,' said Katsuma. 'We've forgotten the frogestra! We need to tempt them out to sing for us.'

Katsuma opened one of the bug jars and emptied it on to the jungle floor.

'Come and get your free insects here!' he yelled.

Out of the darkness, a hundred pairs of yellow eyes snapped opened and the frogs began to sing!

RrrrrrriBIT! RrrrrrrrrrrriBIT! RrriBIT!

'More bugs!' Katsuma called, and the Supers tipped out more insects as fast as the frogs could eat them!

TING! TING! TING! MUUUUUUUUURK! MUUUUUUUUUUURK! MUUUUUURK! BLO-BLO-BLO! PAH! PAH! PAH-PAH! RrrrrrrrrrriBIT!

With the Summoning song in full swing, CocoLoco

hopped from the branch on to the jungle floor and began to jump and jive to the rhythm!

And don't think the Super Moshis ignored the wonderful sounds; everyone was wiggling and jiggling! Well . . . almost everyone.

Buster waited patiently for his chance, a Moshling net poised over CocoLoco until – WHUMP! – he slammed it down. But he was too slow and the nippy Moshling zipped into the undergrowth and disappeared!

'He's escaping! After him!' Buster yelled, running into the jungle with the Supers right on his tail. CocoLoco was fast, but the Super Moshis were only a heartbeat behind.

Suddenly, Zommer caught sight of something glowing in the clearing up ahead. 'Suffering Slimecakes, what's that?!' he cried, grabbing the other Supers and grinding to a halt.

But no one bothered to answer – it was obvious. They'd found the crashed UFO!!

A small figure was underneath the spaceship, tinkering

with the machinery. It heard the Moshis crashing into the clearing and looked up in alarm, before breaking into a huge smile.

'Hello!' it called happily in a singsong voice. 'I'm Captain Squirk, a Zoshling from the planet Symphonia! How very glad I am to meet you!'

He trotted across, his hand extended in greeting, while the Super Moshis, Buster and even CocoLoco gawped in amazement.

'Hello, Captain Squirk,' smiled Poppet as she shook his hand. 'We're the Super Moshis from Monstro City. And this is Buster Bumblechops, the famous Moshling collector.'

Captain Squirk

beamed as he shook
everybody's hand,
including CocoLoco's!

'Our top scientist,
Tamara Tesla, told us
about your ship crash-
landing on Music
Island, so we've come
help you,' explained
Katsuma. 'If you need
help, that is.'

'Cosmic crumbs, yes please!' Squirk said gratefully.
'Come aboard my ship, the *Rhapsody 2*, and we can
talk.' He eyed CocoLoco. 'You can bring your pet
aboard if you wish.'

Buster looked nervously at the Naughty Nutter.

'If it's all the same to you, Captain, I'd like to talk to
CocoLoco about the future,' he explained politely. 'I'm
hoping this Moshling wants to come back to Monstro
City with me.'

CocoLoco jumped up and down with excitement. It seemed the Moshling was indeed keen to go!

Captain Squirk nodded and led the way, scampering up the ladder and into the spacecraft.

Once inside the UFO, the Supers couldn't help but notice how quiet it was!

Where were the robots and the scientists? Where was the crew?

'You've probably already noticed there's no one about,' said Squirk. 'There are usually four of us, but after the crash-landing, my team all went missing on Music Island.'

'Oh, that's awful!' Luvli cried. 'Can't you fly over the island and look for them?'

'The entire crew is needed to power up the *Rhapsody 2*,' explained Squirk. 'It's the fastest ship in the Swooniverse, and one of the most technologically advanced. But it's nothing without my crew, First Officer Ooze, Dr. C. Fingz and Splutnik.'

Captain Squirk looked sadly at the circle of eager

faces surrounding him.

'Let me explain from the beginning,' he said.

The Moshis were listening so carefully that what they didn't notice was a shady figure creeping quietly onto the spaceship, hauling a dirty suitcase behind him.

'Our scientists on Symphonia detected a completely new star orbiting your world. They sent me and my crew to investigate,' explained Squirk. 'We were nearing our destination when the *Rhapsody 2* was sent spinning out of control by what looked like a giant flying glove! We were literally slapped and, unable to recover from such a blow, we crash-landed here!'

'A glove?' Luvli asked.

Squirk nodded.

'What can we do to help, Captain?' asked Poppet.

'My ship's scanners are still working and I've been searching Music Island for Zoshling lifeforms,' replied Squirk. 'When I've found my crew, perhaps I can call on you to guide them back to the ship?'

'Of course, Captain,' said Katsuma. 'Is there nothing we can do in the meantime?'

Captain Squirk smiled sadly and shook his head.

'No, thank you. I will be in contact as soon as I have any news.'

Leaving Captain Squirk to work on his ship, the Moshis headed back outide to fill in Buster Bumblechops on the Zoshling situation.

'A new star orbiting our world? A giant flying glove? A ship slapped out of the sky?' Buster said, shaking his head in disbelief. 'And I thought CocoLoco was crazy! What are you going to do, Super Moshis?'

'Sit tight and wait for the first Zoshling sighting,'

replied Katsuma, with a shrug. 'What are you going to
do with CocoLoco?'

The Super Moshis looked down at the Moshling
as it happily sucked bongo-colada from its nutty head.

'CocoLoco has agreed to come with me back to Monstro City,' beamed Buster, 'where we'll dance the conga all day, every day!'

Chapter 6

HOODOO HIDEAWAY

Captain Squirk frowned as he studied the *Rhapsody 2*'s scanners. They hadn't found any Zoshling life forms on Music Island, but he knew his crew had to be here somewhere!

Sighing loudly, he turned from the computer console to gaze out of the ship's main window.

'What on Symphonia . . . ?' Squirk suddenly gasped.

There, on the outside of the windscreen, a piece of paper flapped in the jungle breeze. It was a note. Less than a minute later, Captain Squirk had summoned the Super Moshis.

SUPER MOSHIS,

THE KEY TO THE ZOSHLING UFO IS BEING HELD AT THE HOODOO HIDEAWAY.

A FRIEND

X

'. . . and you have no idea who taped this to the windscreen?' Katsuma asked, reading the note for the tenth time.

Squirk shrugged. 'No. I didn't realize my ignition key was missing either. But it is.' He pointed at a hole in the control panel.

'This is the only lead we have. Let's go and get this key,' said Diavlo.

Poppet, Luvli and Zommer nodded in agreement, while Furi stuffed his furry face full of Captain Squirk's space sandwiches.

'It's signed "a friend", Katsuma,' said Furi, a fine

shower of breadcrumbs spraying the Supers. 'And it has a kiss on it! I think we can all agree he or she can be trusted, yeah?'

'Of course, we can,' replied Katsuma sarcastically. 'A kiss on an anonymous note makes all the difference!'

'Well then, we're all in agreement,' said Luvli. 'We've got a map of Music Island to help us find the way to the Hoodoo Hideaway, so let's go!'

Katsuma shook his head in disbelief, but the Super Moshis had voted and majority rules!

After some quick reassurances to Captain Squirk that they'd soon return with the Key, the Super Moshis left the *Rhapsody 2* and made their way into the jungle.

'Pfft! Is it just me or is it kind of strange that a hideaway would be marked on a map?' Zommer asked as the Super Moshis trudged along the jungle path.

'Yeah, but I get the impression that Hoodoos might not be the smartest furballs in the foliage,' said Diavlo.

'Oh no, Diavlo, that's where you're wrong,' said Poppet. 'The Hoodoos are as wise as Professor Purplex and as clever as a Tabby Nerdicat. And there's nothing they don't know about the healing arts; they could mix a potion to make even the sleepiest of Silly Snufflers stay awake for a month of Tuesdays! Plus, although they talk to each other by whistling, they're quite able to make themselves understood to us Moshis.'

'And yet they have their hideout clearly marked on a map,' repeated Zommer.

'C'mon, guys,' said Katsuma. 'Less talk, more walk!'

'Mmmmm, I smell something yummy cooking,' said Furi, rubbing his rumbling tummy.

'We must be getting close to Hoodoo Hideaway,' said Poppet.

As faint whistling drifted through the trees, they noticed dozens of bright eyes shining out from the undergrowth.

'Hello!' Zommer bellowed in his best non-threatening manner.

All of a sudden, a furry Woolly Blue Hoodoo appeared before them. A horned skull was jammed on his head and an eyepatch was strung across his face.

'Who you?' he demanded, shaking a skull-tipped staff at the strangers.

'We're the Super Moshis and we've come to . . .

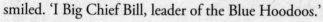

er . . . seek
enlightenment
and learn about
. . . er . . . jungle
medicine?' Luvli
stammered.

'Ahhhh, Hoodoos
always ready to help
strangers,' the Hoodoo
smiled. 'I Big Chief Bill, leader of the Blue Hoodoos.'

While the Super Moshis took turns to shake Bill's furry mitt, little Hoodoos shyly scrambled out of the bushes to check out the new arrivals.

'Welcome to Hoodoo Hideaway,' grinned Big Chief Bill, leading them into the Hoodoos' camp.

'They sure like a decorative skull around here,' whispered Poppet to Diavlo as she gazed around Hoodoo Hideaway. The place was festooned with them: skull lanterns, skull drums, skull staffs, skull knick-knacks of every type!

'And horns,' he replied quietly. 'The horn-and-skull thing does seem popular.'

Suddenly Big Chief Bill appeared at their side.

'Admiring camp, Super Moshis?' He beamed proudly.

Poppet and Diavlo smiled politely in reply.

'I show you Hoodoos' big treasure,' said Bill, trotting off to the far end of the clearing.

He pointed to the chief's throne. On it was perched a green and blue crown.

'Precious Idol-from-the-Sky,' Bill said in awe, gazing up at it.

Diavlo and Poppet exchanged hurried looks. Idol-from-the-Sky? Could this be the Key to the Zoshlings' ship?

'What's it do, Chief?' Poppet asked innocently, trying hard to hide her excitement.

'It give us power over other Hoodoos we no longer friends with,' said Bill.

'And . . . it just fell out of the sky . . . quite recently?' Diavlo asked.

'Why you want to know?' Bill asked sharply.

'Just interested!' sang Poppet. Bill turned back to look at the 'crown', while Poppet elbowed Diavlo in the ribs. 'Drop it,' she whispered. 'He's getting suspicious, but I've got an idea. If we patch up the Hoodoo friendship problem, the Blue Hoodoos won't need the Key!' Luvli said. 'And they'll owe us . . .'

Later, at Hoodoo teatime, the Super Moshis finally found out why these Hoodoos were arguing with the other Hoodoos. Or 'Hoodudes', as Big Chief Bill called them. It appeared to have started when the Hoodudes' Green Honcho accused Big Chief Bill of

sitting on his hat. Bill insisted that the Green Honcho had purposely slipped it under his bottom.

'Only when Hoodoo tribes have big, big party and feast on ancient Hot Hoodoo Stew will fighting stop,' said Bill wistfully.

'Well, let's make this stew then!' Diavlo cried.

'Too difficult,' said Bill. 'I show.'

With a clap of his hands a Hoodoo appeared before them and Bill gave his instructions. Soon the Hoodoo was back, clutching a large dusty book.

'Hoodoo book of recipes,' Bill explained. Finding the page, he passed the book to Katsuma who read aloud:

'*Hot Hoodoo Stew has been carefully crafted* . . . blah blah blah . . . *to unite splintered Hoodoo tribes* . . . yadda yadda . . . *Each tribe is responsible for one ingredient that cannot be found anywhere else.*'

'Problem here. When arguing, we no share ingredient,' said Bill sadly.

The Super Moshis exchanged looks and grinned.

'We think we can help, Chief,' beamed Luvli.
'Let us collect the ingredients for the Hoodoo Stew.
What do you say?'

Log in to **MOSHIMONSTERS.COM**, click the **ENTER SECRET CODE** button and type the **first word** on the **tenth line** on **page 77**. Your surprise free gift will appear in your treasure chest!

Chapter 7

SEARCHING FOR OOBLA DOOBLA

As Katsuma trudged through the jungle, he thought over how events had unfolded at Hoodoo Hideaway the previous evening.

It hadn't taken a genius to work out that Big Chief Bill was desperate to put an end to the disagreement between the Hoodoo tribes, so it was no surprise to the Super Moshis that he'd jumped at the offer of their help.

'The Oobla Doobla come from SnaggleTooth Swamp of Orange Hoodoos,' explained Bill. 'You find coconut shells there too maybe. Purple

bananas from Walla Walla Watering Hole, home of
Green Hoodudes. And creepy crawlies.' Here Bill had
paused and smacked his lips hungrily. 'Tomorrow we

go into Unknown Zone where bestest creepy crawlies live. After that, you on your own.'

But before Big Chief Bill would trust them with the sacred Hoodoo book of recipes, the Super Moshis had had to prove themselves worthy by successfully performing a series of challenges. Luckily none of the tests had been too difficult!

In fact, Zommer had so totally ruled the Hoodoo Pongoo game challenge that he'd won every game!

Katsuma's daydreaming was interrupted by Zommer muttering. 'I hope we get to wherever we're going soon. This walking is quite literally knocking the stuffing out of me!'

Katsuma looked round and winced as he saw bits of grass and sawdust leaking out of a hole in Zommer's side where his stitches had come loose.

'Pull yourself together, Zom!' Katsuma laughed.

'Could you darn me?' Zommer chuckled. 'Cos sometimes you can be a total sew-and-sew, Katsuma!'

Big Chief Bill raised his hand and the Super Moshis

came to a halt.

'Here creepy-crawly smorgasbord!' said Bill.

'We need one cupful of creepy crawlies,' Poppet said, reading from the recipe book. 'So pick the best ones. We want this stew to be the greatest thing these Hoodoos have ever tasted!'

'I feel like a contestant on MonsterChef!' Zommer laughed, as the Supers spread out to look for bugs.

Furi murmured happily to himself as he searched through the forest.

'One for the stew pot,' he said, pulling a fat worm out of the ground and popping it into a jar. 'And one for me.'

CRUNCH! CRUNCH!

Furi's mouth watered as he bit down on the crispy shell of a beetle.

Big Chief Bill was right – there were so many creepy crawlies in this part of the Unknown Zone, the Super Moshis had found enough for ten Hoodoo Stews!

But time was short and the Supers had the next ingredient to collect.

'You find Oobla Doobla in SnaggleTooth Swamp,' Bill said as Poppet stowed the jars of bugs in her backpack. 'Woolly Orange Hoodoos live there, so Bill not go. You take map, you find easy. But before you go . . .'

Bill hesitated.

'What is it, Chief?' Diavlo asked.

Big Chief Bill puffed out his cheeks and fiddled with his eye patch.

'Super Moshis already help Blue Hoodoos,' he began timidly. 'Bill don't want to push his luck . . .'

But it was obvious he was itching to ask the Super Moshis something!

'If we can do anything for you, Chief . . . ?' Zommer said.

'There shiny frog in pond. It ruin balance of nature,' Bill blurted, clearly relieved to get it off his furry blue chest. 'Bad juju for Hoodoo!'

'So . . . you want us to get rid of this frog?' Katsuma asked.

The Woolly Blue Hoodoo nodded vigorously.

The pond had a silvery sheen, smelt like rotten eggs and its water was green and murky.

'All right, guys. Let's bag this toxic nuisance and . . . oh, grooooovy!' Diavlo fell silent as he caught sight of a frog crouched on a rock on the far side of the pond. It shone like a torch in the semi-darkness of the jungle.

'Dudes! Is that frog *glowing*?' Furi gasped in amazement.

Luvli turned to Bill.

'How did the frog get here, Chief?' she asked.

'Many year ago frog appear,' began Bill. 'He found sitting on top of singing microwave which sing and sing and sing, till one day it disappear – probably snatched by greedy Orange Hoodoos! But frog, he stay. His shiny skin make pond sick. All other creatures go. So you take frog, creatures come back and pond get well.'

The Super Moshis studied the frog, which gazed back at them with unblinking eyes.

'I'm pretty sure our little froggy friend over there is emitting nuclear energy,' said Poppet suddenly, 'which explains the stagnant pond water and the unnatural glow of the plants!'

'In which case,' said Zommer, flexing his gloved hand. 'Everyone stand back and leave it to the expert. Poppet, pass me the bag, please.'

The nuclear frog blinked disinterestedly as Zommer skirted the stinky pool and grabbed it, popping it into a hessian sack without a fight!

The only problem came on the return journey,

when Zommer lost his balance on the slippery bank and tumbled head first into the greasy water!

'You've got pond scum in your hair, Zom,' Furi pointed out as Zommer hauled himself back on to the pond's bank.

'Yeah! It makes excellent hair gel!' Zommer grinned, shaping his pink locks into stiff points.

Mini mission accomplished, it was time for Big Chief Bill to return to Hoodoo Hideaway.

'Thank you, Super Moshis. You good friends to Blue Hoodoos,' he said. 'You get Oobla Doobla and rest of ingredients and you come back to Hoodoo Hideaway soon, OK?'

'We'll do our best, Chief,' smiled Furi.

'Welcome, weary wanderers!' The Orange Hoodoo chief bustled forward as the Super Moshis trooped into SnaggleTooth Swamp.

'Hi, we're the Super Moshis,' said Katsuma as he

shook the little Woolly Hoodoo by the fuzzy hand. 'We were wondering if you could spare a little Oobla Doobla . . .'

'Help yourself to as much as you want,' said the Orange Hoodoo, pointing to the masses of green gourds hanging from the vines criss-crossing the swamp. 'But Oobla Doobla . . . it's not to everyone's taste . . .'

'It's not for us,' explained Diavlo. 'We're brewing up a batch of hot Hoodoo Stew.'

'You are?' the Orange Hoodoo said in astonishment. 'Does this mean the Green and Blue Hoodoos want to put an end to the fighting between our tribes?'

'Yes! Big Chief Bill is throwing a massive party and you're all invited! But first we have to collect the ingredients,' replied Poppet.

She pulled the Hoodoo book of recipes out of her backpack and showed the Orange Hoodoo.

'One. Fried. Oobla. Doobla,' said the Orange Hoodoo slowly, his finger tracing the words as he read them. 'Hey, Super Moshis, you realize you'll need to

cook that Oobla Doobla?'

'*What*?' Diavlo dived on the book and read it himself. 'He's right! How are we going to fry the Oobla Doobla when we're in the middle of the jungle?'

The Orange Hoodoo boss burst out laughing.

'If only you'd arrived a few days ago,' he giggled. 'I had a singing microwave, but the thing wouldn't shut up! It warbled the same annoying tune, day in, day out!

So, in the end . . . '

He pointed to a smashed-up microwave half hanging out of a nearby tree.

The Super Moshis groaned in dismay.

'If you can fix, you can use,' the Orange Hoodoo said with a shrug.

'Hold on a second,' said Katsuma. 'Did you say a singing microwave? We captured a nuclear frog back at a smelly old pond and apparently it mysteriously appeared one day with a singing microwave . . .' Katsuma trailed off.

'What a . . . er . . . coincidence.' The Orange Hoodoo looked uncomfortable and quickly changed the subject. 'Soooo, while you're here, could you

Supers do me a favour? I've got some old tin cans messing up the swamp. Can you help me get rid of them?'

Diavlo turned to his friends.

'We may as well help him while we decide what we're going to do about the Oobla Doobla situ,' he said.

The others nodded in agreement.

'T'riffic! This way, Super Moshis,' cried the Orange Hoodoo happily.

'I . . . I . . . I can't believe it!'

'I don't believe it!'

'What are those two metallic morons doing in there?'

The Super Moshis were all talking at once as they eyed a pair of unhappy robots submerged up to their necks in the grotty waters of SnaggleTooth Swamp.

'You know them?' the Orange Hoodoo asked.

'Yes! They're Sprockett and Hubbs, master inventors for our arch-enemy, C.L.O.N.C.,' Poppet explained. 'The last time we saw them their master was attempting to destroy Monstro City using a weapon they'd invented!'

Chapter 8

SPROCKETT AND HUBBS HELP OUT

'When we're finished with you two, there'll be nothing left but scrap metal!' Diavlo said, steaming menacingly.

'Wait, Super Moshis,' pleaded Hubbs. 'We're not working for C.L.O.N.C. any more! They kicked us off Scare Force One when our SuperWeapon . . . er . . . failed to perform . . .'

'Spit it out, you gas-guzzling goofball!' Sprockett snapped. 'He means our SuperWeapon malfunctioned so they pushed us out of the plane as we flew over Music Island. Hence our present problem.'

'This is just another one of your tricks!' Katsuma snorted in disbelief.

'It's true!' Hubbs cried. 'Please get us out of this swamp. This green goo is gunging up my gaskets!'

'We should get them out of there,' sighed Luvli. 'They might give us a lead on where to find Elder Furi.'

The others grunted in reluctant agreement. But the problem was how to get two heavy robots out of the thick gooey swamp . . .?

'How about we form a Super Moshi chain,' suggested Poppet. 'Then use this large branch over here on the ground and –'

Suddenly, the 'tree branch' Poppet was pointing at rolled over in the mud.

'ARRRRRRRGHHHHH! Croc!' Poppet screamed.

The Super Moshis leapt back as the Orange Hoodoo rolled on the ground laughing hysterically.

'That's my pet crocodile, Dundee!' the Orange Hoodoo hooted. 'He was just having his afternoon nap. He won't hurt you.'

Dundee the crocodile yawned widely, closing his jaws again with an audible snap!

'This croc gives me an idea,' said Katsuma, eyeing Dundee warily. 'He's easily the strongest one here, so how about we use him to pull Sprockett and Hubbs out of the swamp? We could tie a vine to the robots and

get ol' Dundee to yank them out.'

'And how exactly do we get a crocodile to pull a vine?' Furi asked doubtfully.

'Coax him with food,' said the Orange Hoodoo.

'HEAVE!' SHLUUUUUUUUUUUUUUUUUPP!

Out popped Sprockett.

'HEAVE!' SHLUUUUUUUUUUUUUUPP! Out popped Hubbs.

While Dundee gobbled up the rest of his Oobla Doobla treats, the Super Moshis tipped the mud-encrusted robots upright on dry land.

'Thanks, Super Moshis,' said Sprockett gratefully. 'If only there was some way we could prove to you that we're good guys now . . .'

'We don't trust you crates of cogs an inch,' frowned Furi. 'But you can start by fixing a broken microwave oven.'

'No problem!'

said Sprokett and Hobbs together, and they set about repairing the machine.

In no time at all it was good as new, and only needed a power source to get it going again.

'So what do we have? Batteries? Solar power? Petrol generator . . . ?' Hubbs asked the Orange Hoodoo.

'How about a nuclear frog?' Diavlo suggested with a wink.

'Should do the trick,' replied Sprockett, barely raising an electronic eyebrow.

Zommer fished the glowing creature from the sack and popped it on top of the microwave. The machine shook and hummed and with a 'ding!' came back to life.

'Let's fry some Oobla Doobla!' cried Katsuma, shoving the plant inside.

As soon as it was cooked, Katsuma stored the Oobla Doobla safely in his backpack, while Poppet studied the map.

'Where to next?' he asked, peering over her shoulder.

'Walla Walla Watering Hole,' she replied. 'That's where the purple bananas are.'

'I suppose those tin twits will be tagging along?'

Poppet looked over at Sprockett and Hubbs, who were already arguing with Zommer and Furi, and sighed. 'I guess so . . . '

Luvli and Diavlo soared high over the treetops, watching the Supers and Sprockett and Hubbs as they threaded their way along the rough jungle track.

'I don't trust them one bit,' snarled Diavlo, eyeing the ex-C.L.O.N.C. baddies. 'They're mercenaries! Inventors for hire! They'd do anything as long as there were Rox in it for them.'

'They're also bungling idiots,' replied Luvli.

'Their story about getting
kicked off Scare Force
One because
of a weapons
malfunction . . .
that sounded
genuine.'

Diavlo snorted
and looked down
suspiciously at
the bungling
robots.

'Even so,
having them along on this
trip to Walla Walla Watering Hole makes me nervous.
They could be hatching a plot to trick us,' he said.
'I'd feel a lot better if we knew where Dr. Strangeglove
was . . .'

Down below in the depths of the steamy jungle, Furi was having the same doubts as Diavlo.

'There's only one way to gain our complete trust,' said Furi, poking Sprockett in the back. 'Tell us where Strangeglove is.'

Sprockett groaned.

'How many times do we have to say this? We don't know!'

'As my ridiculous robotic friend here has already explained a zillion times,' cut in Hubbs. 'Dr. Strangeglove was kicked off Scare Force One too. He'd done something to upset the head of C.L.O.N.C. and he was ejected just like we were.'

'So he's here? On Music Island?' Katsuma asked.

'We. Don't. Know!' Sprockett said slowly, stressing every syllable.

Questioning the robots was getting the Super Moshis nowhere!

'Well, just so you know, any false moves and you guys are going straight back into the swamp,' said Poppet.

As she spoke, a big stone got caught in Hubbs's rollerball wheel, sending him skidding off the track in the direction of a large muddy bog that ran alongside the path. But Poppet quickly realized it wasn't a bog; it was quicksand! Anything that went in would be sucked under and never seen again!

'Hurry, Katsuma!' Poppet yelled. 'If he goes in there, it's goodnight, Hubbs!'

Katsuma's paw shot forward and he grabbed Hubbs by his metal fingertips, hauling him back on to the track.

'Thank you,' said Hubbs huffily. 'That was quick thinking – for a hare-brained Moshi.'

'Who are you calling hare-brained?' scowled Katsuma.

'Well, you are a type of rabbit, aren't you?' Hubbs muttered as he continued down the path.

Nearby at the Walla Walla Watering Hole, the natives

were holding a Hoodoo powwow.

At the foot of their giant Hoodoo idol, the Green Hoodoo Honcho perched silently while his right-hand man, Kook, addressed the Hoodoo horde.

'As you all know, someone has been messing about with the Walla Walla Water Monument and nicked off with three vital pieces of stone work,' said Kook. 'If we don't find them in time, our sacred watering hole will drain of water and you all know what that means!'

'No surfing!' the Green Hoodudes intoned sadly.

'And that would be . . . what?' Kook asked.

'A major bummer!' the crowd chanted in reply.

'Totally, dudes,' agreed Kook. 'In which case we need to get our search on, pronto! So if the Hoodoos of –'

'Bombs away!' Furi hollered behind Kook, flinging himself into the cool, clean waters of the watering hole.

'Right behind you, Furi!' Zommer laughed as he belly-flopped into the sacred waters with a loud **THWACK!**

'Hey, stranger-dudes! That is so not cool!' Kook yelled as the crowd swarmed over to the waterhole's edge.

The remaining Supers on the opposite bank watched in dismay as the Green Hoodoos shook their fists angrily at Zommer and Furi splashing happily in the sacred waters.

Sprockett snickered nastily.

'Way to make friends with the Green Hoodoos, Super Saps!' Hubbs laughed. 'You'll never get those purple bananas now!'

HIIIIII-YAH! Katsuma let fly with a roundhouse instep kick, sending Hubbs speeding down the bank and into the lake.

'That's for calling me hare-brained, you glass-headed gasbag!' Katsuma called after him as Hubbs disappeared under the water.

Chapter 9

SURF'S UP

The banks of the lake were so steep that Hubbs didn't stop rolling until he reached the very bottom of the water! The sun's rays barely reached so deep and Hubbs found himself in semi-darkness.

'Don't panic,' he muttered to himself as he bobbed along the lakebed. 'I'll look around. There's got to be something down here to help me escape this scandalous situation.'

In the murky half-light he saw a pile of rocks.

'Perhaps I could use those to build an exit ramp . . . ?'

Wheeling over to investigate, he noticed that the three stones at the top of the pile were perfectly round and intricately carved.

'That's weird! Why would the Green Hoodoos go to the trouble of decorating these big bits of rock only

to throw them to the bottom of the – OOOOF!'

Something slammed into Hubbs's head. He turned to find a large surfboard dangling from a long green vine, which snaked along the lakebed and up, up, up the steep bank until it disappeared into the air above.

'A typical Super Moshi rescue attempt,' he scoffed, clumsily climbing aboard. 'Designed to provide maximum humiliation!'

The surfboard began to rise to the surface as the Super Moshis and Hoodoos on shore worked together to haul the robot to safety.

Watched by a handful of curious Green Hoodoo kiddies (who'd never seen a robot before), Hubbs dried off while Sprockett filled him in on what had happened while he'd been at the bottom of the lake.

'That little Green Hoodude, Kook, was furious with Furi and Zommer for jumping into the Hoodoos' sacred lake,' explained Sprockett. 'But after Katsuma explained how hot and dirty everyone was after traipsing through the jungle and about the Hoodoo Stew and the party the Blue Hoodoos are throwing and the truce and the – '

'Yeah, I get it,' snapped Hubbs, unscrewing his helmet and emptying the water out of it. The young Hoodoos squealed in delight – the tin can had pulled off its own head! 'And where are those beastly Moshi meddlers now?'

'They're helping the Green Hoodoos find some pieces of an idol they've lost or something,' replied Sprockett, playfully swatting away a pair of little Hoodoos who'd ventured closer.

'Pieces of an idol?' Hubbs yelped, suddenly interested. 'Did they say what these pieces looked like?'

'Uh . . . Kook said round with carved bits, I think,' said Sprockett doubtfully. A slow smile spread across Hubbs's face as he remembered the 'stones' at the bottom of the lake.

'In that case we'd better find this Kook,' he chuckled. 'I'll explain on the way. But let's just say I can smell a reward . . .'

Sprockett and Hubbs (and their Hoodoo kiddy entourage) caught up with the Super Moshis and Kook a little way out of the camp.

'Mr Kook!' Hubbs called, wheeling up to him. 'I think I –'

'Push off, wheelie bin.' Zommer interrupted with a frown.

'But I found the missing p –'

'Do you want to go back into the lake?' Katsuma asked.

'Now that you come to mention it –' Hubbs managed to say before Diavlo cut him off.

'Go back to Walla Walla Watering Hole and wait for us there,' he barked.

The more the Supers refused to listen to Hubbs,

the angrier Sprockett
became. Soon his
circuits began to
smoke and his antenna
started to fizzle; no one
was allowed to speak
to Hubbs like that . . .
except him!

'HUBBS KNOWS
WHERE TO FIND
THE MISSING
PIECES OF THE
IDOL!' he roared, sending the little Hoodoos
scurrying into the bushes for cover.

The jungle fell deathly quiet as the Green Hoodoos,
the Super Moshis and Hubbs all turned to stare
at Sprockett.

'I was just sayin',' he mumbled in an embarrassed
voice. Everyone stood around the edge of the lake and
watched as Hubbs prepared to retrieve the missing

pieces of the Water Monument.

'Trust those Super Moshis to send me back down there,' whined Hubbs as Sprockett checked the knots on the vine that was tied round Hubbs's waist.

'It does mean we'll get to keep the entire reward that Kook talked about,' said Sprockett with a shrug.

'Bah! Easy for you to say! You're not the one getting water in your circuit boards! AGAIN!'

'Ready, Hubbs?' Furi called. 'We'll winch you down and then you tie the vine round the first piece of idol and we'll pull it to the surface. We'll do this three times and then on the fourth we'll haul you up. OK?'

'Yes!' Hubbs called, giving the Super Moshis the thumbs-up sign. 'The reward better be worth it,' he muttered darkly to Sprockett.

By the time Hubbs was hauled, coughing and spluttering, to the surface again, the Green Hoodoos had rebuilt their Water Monument and the lake was saved.

'That was totally gnarly, dude,' exclaimed Kook,

slapping Hubbs on the back. 'If it hadn't been for you finding those pieces, we wouldn't have been able to fix the Monument and then the lake would've drained and there'd have been no more surfing! WHEW! And we Green Hoodudes like nothing more than to Hang Ten! Except maybe eating Hoodoo Stew.' Kook turned to Poppet. 'Which reminds me, we'd like you to have these,' he said, handing her a vine of purple bananas. 'We're totally up for the party at the Hoodoo Hideaway. Please tell Bill we said so!'

It was time for the Super Moshis to return to Hoodoo Hideaway. They'd bowed solemnly to the Green Hoodoo Honcho and were bumping fists with Kook when Hubbs wheeled forward and coughed meaningfully.

'Er . . . about that reward . . . ?' he asked shyly.

Kook slapped his forehead. 'Dude, sorry, I almost forgot!' He caught the Green Hoodoo Honcho's eye and the chief nodded gravely. 'The Hoodoo Honcho has bestowed on you our greatest honour . . .'

He clapped his hands and the Honcho's attendants appeared with covered platters balanced on their heads. The Hoodoo kiddies whooped and shouted with excitement.

Hubbs nudged Sprockett and whispered, 'This is gonna be good.'

The platters were ceremoniously laid at the feet of the robots and with a flourish Kook whipped off their covers.

'*Coconut shells?*' Hubbs spluttered in astonishment as he looked at the husks piled high on the platters in front of him.

'Dude, I know, right?' Kook grinned and nodded. 'We've made you and Sprockett honorary Green Hoodudes. This gives you the right to wear the sacred coconut shells.'

Hubbs was speechless, his mouth opening and closing mutely.

'No need to thank us, dude,' said Kook, giving both

robots a hug. 'We owe you the thanks.'

Katsuma and Poppet stepped forward and hastily stowed the coconuts in their backpacks as Luvli hovered at Hubbs's shoulder.

'We need those coconut shells for the Hoodoo Stew,' she hissed. 'Just say thank you and we can go.'

'Thank you,' Hubbs croaked.

Sprockett barely noticed; he was too busy high-fiving his new little Hoodude fan club!

Chapter 10

THE BIG COOK-OFF

'You back!' Big Chief Bill cried as the Super Moshis, Sprockett and Hubbs finally stumbled into the clearing of Hoodoo Hideaway. 'You got ingredient no problem?'

'Not only have we got everything for the Hoodoo Stew,' grinned Katsuma, 'we've talked to the chiefs of the Green and Orange tribes and they can't wait to stop arguing and start partying!'

Grinning broadly, Bill clapped his hands to summon his Hoodoo subjects.

'Let preparations begin! When sun go down, party

start up!' he ordered, before noticing Sprockett and Hubbs. He pointed at them and added, 'And put these ice dispensers somewhere.'

There was a lot to organize and very little time in which to do it, but everyone was willing to help out – although some were more willing than others . . .

The Super Moshis received a crash course in playing the Hoodoo Rallying Cry that would summon the Green and Orange Hoodoos to the festivities.

Soon they were beating out the tune on Hoodoo drums made of skulls and the bark of trees found in the Wobbly Wood.

'Our mission is almost over,' said Katsuma. 'When the party finishes, the fighting will be over and the Blue Hoodoos won't need their precious Idol-from-the-Sky.'

The Super Moshis gazed over at what they hoped was the *Rhapsody 2*'s ignition Key sitting on top of the

Blue Hoodoo throne. Soon it would be returned to its rightful owner . . .

In another part of the camp, Sprockett and Hubbs had a less glamorous job. They'd been put in charge of cleaning out the sacred cauldron used to brew the Hoodoo Stew. It was a big job – the pot hadn't been scrubbed since the last peace party when Big Chief Bill had still been a tiny, fuzzy Hoodoo kiddy in nappies!

'I'd rather be neck-deep in SnaggleTooth Swamp than cleaning out this revolting pot,' grumbled Sprockett as he scraped ancient black grease from the inside of the cauldron.

'And I'd rather be at the bottom of the Whatever Whatever Watering Hole without a surfboard lifeline,' whined Hubbs, a black streak of soot smeared across his glass helmet.

The Blue Hoodoo overseeing them snorted.

'Less blubbing, more scrubbing!' he ordered.

The Green Hoodoo horde were the first to arrive, with the Orange Hoodoos not far behind them. Then bit by bit the jungle shadows began to lengthen as the sun dipped lower in the sky.

The Super Moshis were just wondering what time the party was going to kick off when suddenly a cry went up around Hoodoo Hideaway.

'HOOOOOOODOOOOOOO!
HOOOOOOODOOOOOOO!'

Big Chief Bill strode into the main clearing, with the Green Head Honcho on his left and the Orange Woolly Hoodoo boss on his right.

Behind them the sacred-cauldron bearers carried the now-sparkling pot upon their shoulders. They hung it up over the roaring fire in the middle of the clearing.

'Gather round, friends!' Bill called, gesturing for the crowd to form a large circle round the cauldron. 'This great day for Hoodoo everywhere! Without

Super Moshis we no have Hoodoo Stew, we no have party and we no be friends. So without further ado – let's brew!'

The Hoodoos broke into excited cheers as Bill shouted, 'Bring forth sacred stirring stick!'

Luvli and Diavlo, hovering above the throng, watched as a Blue Hoodoo raced up the steps of the throne and collected the 'sacred stirring stick' lying at its foot. It looked familiar – the shape of the wood, the feathers, the jewel . . .

'Whoa! Isn't that Elder Furi's staff?' Luvli whispered. 'He had it when he disappeared. Which means he must've been here recently!'

'Lardy Lavacakes! I think you're right!' Diavlo whispered in reply.

The two Super Moshis wasted no time in telling the others.

Meanwhile, Big Chief Bill was busy flinging the ingredients for the Hoodoo Stew into the cauldron.

'Stir the pot! Stir the pot!' the Hoodoo tribes

chanted as Bill was handed Elder Furi's staff.

As the chief plunged it deep into the cauldron, a series of huge explosions suddenly rocked Hoodoo Hideaway – **BOOM! BOOM! BOOM!**

The Super Moshis ran for cover behind the Blue Hoodoos' throne, while the Hoodoos' cheers grew louder with every explosion.

Suddenly, though, their excited cries turned angry.

'What's going on?' Poppet yelled. But they soon understood. Frightened by the loud explosions, the Idol-from-the-Sky had scampered down the steps of the throne and was escaping into the jungle!

'The *Rhapsody 2*'s Key is getting away!' shouted Katsuma. 'After it, Super Moshis!'

'The Idol-from-the-Sky flees – run, Hoodoos, RUN!' Big Chief Bill yelled.

The humid air was filled with the sound of hundreds of pairs of feet racing through the jungle.

'The Sixty-two Guardians of Gombala Gombala Jungle will have revenge, Idol!' Big Chief Bill hollered as he sprinted after the Key. 'You no escape!'

The rest of the Hoodoo horde followed close behind their leader, while further back the Super Moshis brought up the rear.

'What's happening, Luvli, can you see?' Poppet managed to ask between gasping breaths.

Luvli and Diavlo, who'd been flying high above them, dropped down to give a report.

'The Hoodoos are gaining on the Key! It looks as if – wait! The Key has tripped over! The Hoodoos have stopped and they're surrounding it – hurry!'

By the time the Super Moshis caught up with the Hoodoos an ominous hush had fallen over the crowd. Leading the way, Katsuma pushed through the Hoodoo horde to the centre of the circle. There he

found the terrified figure of Woolly the Titchy-tusked Mammoth lying flat on his back, with the Key beside him. Big Chief Bill stood, hands on hips, silently staring down at Woolly.

Everyone held their breath – what would Bill say?

'This no idol, this Moshling!' Bill said with surprise. 'Whole time we think this sacred idol . . . and whole time . . . it M-M-M-Moshling!' He paused and looked around at the Hoodoo tribes. '**AHAHAHAHAHA!** This best peace-party practical joke EVER!'

The Hoodoos erupted in gleeful cheers as Bill let out a loud whoop of excitement and turned, leading the reunited tribes back to Hoodoo Hideaway – conga-ing all the way!

Luvli landed softly and helped Woolly to his feet. The poor little Moshling looked frightened half to death!

'It's OK little Woolly, you're perfectly safe now.

Those crazy Hoodoos have gone,' she crooned gently, smoothing his fur. 'You come back to Monstro City with us. Buster Bumblechops will take very good care of you and you'll have lots of other Moshlings to play with.'

Woolly nuzzled Luvli contentedly as the Super Moshis looked at each other and grinned – they'd done it! They finally had the Key!

Zommer picked it up.

'I don't get it,' he said, scratching his head. 'Do the Hoodoos want their Idol back or not?'

It was a full day's march through the Gombala Gombala Jungle before the Super Moshis made it back to the *Rhapsody 2* and were able to tell a relieved Captain Squirk their story.

'...and when we left Hoodoo Hideaway this morning, Big Chief Bill gave us Elder Furi's staff as a souvenir of our time in jungle,' giggled Poppet, holding the staff – which was of course Captain Sqirk's key. 'It'd fallen from the sky – just like their "Idol" – so he didn't want it any more!'

Across from her, Captain Squirk sat open-mouthed in wonder as he absent-mindedly patted Woolly.

'I know! It was a pretty crazy adventure, eh?' Diavlo said, taking another space sandwich.

'You can say that again!' Captain Squirk smiled.

'It was some crazy adv–'

'Not now, Zommer!' the Super Moshis all yelled at once.

Outside in the clearing, Sprockett and Hubbs worked on the *Rhapsody 2*. The crash-landing had damaged some of the ship's vital functions and the two robots were putting their expertise to work.

'Now be careful what you're doing this time, Hubbs,' snapped Sprockett. 'We don't want a repeat performance of what happened on Scare Force One.'

'It wasn't me that caused that weapons malfunction,' complained Hubbs. 'It was your shoddy work that did it!'

'HA! I'm the one with the degree in Moshi Microprocessing and –'

The arguing continued late into the afternoon . . .

Back in Monstro City, Tamara Tesla clicked her Moshi Minifone shut.

'Thank the stars Katsuma called to let me know about the crashed spaceship from Symphonia,' she muttered to herself. 'That's the UFO problem solved.'

She bit her lip and looked worriedly at the space scans on her desk. 'But now we have a bigger problem. A new star in the Swooniverse – one that's getting bigger by the day.'

Her antennae zapped and crackled while she performed difficult calculations. The metallic smell of electricity filled the air. A new star this close to the Moshis' own world could prove disastrous for Monstro City; it could affect the weather patterns, the temperature, the . . . wait . . . that reminded her of something.

Tamara darted over to her filing cabinet and yanked open a drawer.

'Yes, here it is,' she said, fishing out the *Daily Growl* article she'd carefully saved from the previous week.

'There's something very strange happening in the

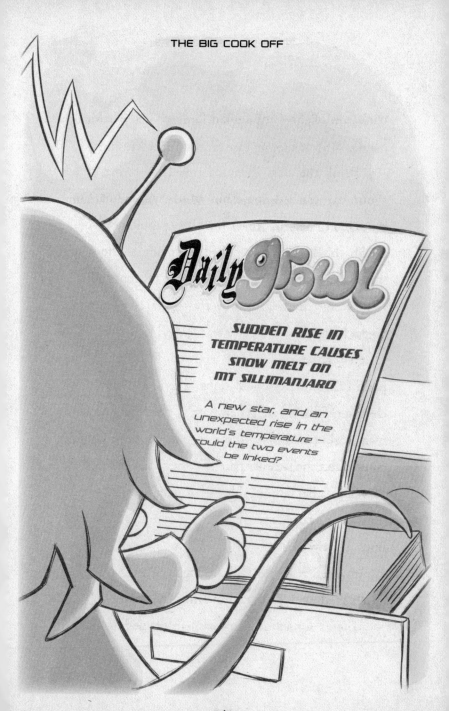

Way-Outta-Sphere,' whispered Tamara Tesla, looking up at the sky. 'This is another case for the Super Moshis!'

*The action continues in **Music Island Missions: C.L.O.N.C. Strikes Back!***

Don't miss the next exciting Music Island Mission adventure, coming soon in paperback and ebook:

Read an exclusive extract on the next page!

Chapter 1

C.L.O.N.C. STRIKES AGAIN

Deep in the jungle on Music Island, aboard a crash-landed spaceship, Captain Squirk looked up from the scans he'd been studying and frowned thoughtfully at the Super Moshis.

'I've some good news . . . and some bad news,' said the tiny Zoshling. 'The good news is the *Rhapsody 2*'s ZPS has located one of my missing crew members. If you can rescue my friend, that only leaves two more Zoshlings to find! Then, the *Rhapsody 2* can take off again and investigate this new star in the Grosshead Nebula system.'

'Where does the ZPS say this Zoshling is?' asked

Katsuma excitedly, ignoring the bit about the star.

'Somewhere called the Sandy Drain Hotel,' said Squirk, scratching his head.

The Super Moshis exchanged astonished looks. What would a Zoshling from the planet Symphonia be doing at *the* celebrity hotspot on Music Island? Wow. They were going to do some serious star-spotting!

'Don't forget the bad news,' Squirk reminded them, waggling his finger. The Super Moshis' grins vanished. 'That new star I told you about? It's getting bigger.'

'Bigger? How is that possible?' asked Luvli, her fluttery eyes widening.

'I don't know.' Squirk shook his head. 'Worse, super scientist Tamara Tesla called to say it seems to be melting the snow on Mount Sillimanjaro. Melted snow means the sea levels are rising . . . and Monstro City is in danger of drowning!'

The Super Moshis gasped in unison.

'Super Moshis,' pleaded Captain Squirk, 'you must return all my Zoshling crew as soon as possible so we can lift off and solve this interstellar puzzle – before it's too late!'

'We'll leave for the Sandy Drain Hotel at once, Captain,' said Poppet gravely. 'You can count on us.'

'Stop it, Furi,' hissed Diavlo out of the corner of his mouth. 'What are you doing digging about in those pot plants?'

Furi stumbled away from the little garden outside the reception of the famous Sandy Drain Hotel.

'I'm feeling peckish,' he replied. 'I was just looking for some grubs.'

'Well, don't,' scolded Diavlo. 'It's embarrassing. This is an eight-star hotel, not the Gombala Gombala Jungle! We have to act *cool*. We have to act with *decorum*. We have to –'

'Hey, Furi! Check this out!' Zommer yelled as he whizzed round and round inside a huge brass revolving door.

'That. Is. AWESOME!' Furi squealed, rushing towards the grand entrance to join in the fun.

'Gah!' said Diavlo, slapping his forehead. 'I give up!'

Diavlo, Poppet, Katsuma and Luvli ushered Furi and Zommer through the door and into the swanky lobby. The Moshis gaped at the groovy purple walls and funky furniture.

'Wow!' Poppet exclaimed. 'This is so cool!'

'Isn't it? It's going to be full of celebrities,' Luvli sighed as she spied Taylor Miffed relaxing on a sofa in the corner.

'OK, OK. Don't lose it!' Katsuma warned. 'Remember, we're here on a mission. We have to find this Zoshling and return it to the *Rhapsody 2* – and quickly. So let me handle this.'

He set off across the plush lilac carpet towards the reception desk. He'd only taken half a dozen steps when someone grabbed his arm.

'What are you lot doing here?' Simon Growl snapped. 'I hope you aren't going to cause any more trouble.'

'Trouble?' Katsuma frowned. 'Oh, if you're talking about that hot little incident on your Sneerjet —'

Simon Growl's hair growled.

'Well, we've already apologized for that. It's not like we cause havoc everywhere we go.'

The words were barely out of Katsuma's mouth before he heard an almighty crash behind him. The crowded hotel lobby fell silent. Turning slowly, he saw Furi and Zommer sprawled on the floor, cackling gleefully. They'd flown out of the revolving door, hit several pot plants mid-air and crashed to the ground. Wet soil was scattered across the pristine purple carpet.

'You were saying, Katsuma?' Growl snickered. His hair chortled too.

Katsuma stared at the mess, speechless.

'Are these . . . creatures . . . friends of yooooooours, Mr Growl?' boomed an annoyed voice.

Katsuma turned away from his embarrassing friends to find a large, smartly dressed cow looming over him. Her jaw flapped uncontrollably.

'Nope,' he replied. 'I'll be sunbathing if anyone needs me, Frau BrownKau. Ciao!' And with that he scarpered off to the pool.

Frau Now BrownKau, the manager of the Sandy Drain Hotel, focused her withering gaze on Katsuma.

'Can I help yooooou with anything?' she drawled haughtily, her teeth chomping. Pain creased her features every time she spoke.

'Er, yes. We'd like a room, please,' Katsuma said nervously. The rest of the Super Moshis gathered around behind him. 'For all of us.'

'That will beeeeeeee five million Rox… per night,' Frau Now BrownKau winced.

'*What*? Are you kidding?' Diavlo gasped. 'No one could afford that!'

'Our prices ensure we keeeeeeep the riff-raff out,' snapped BrownKau, looking the Super Moshis up and down, her jaw jerking wildly in all directions.

'Look, I don't mean to be rude, love, but is there something wrong with your mouth?' Zommer asked.

'I can't help but notice your gnashers working overtime in there.'

'My teeeeeeeth don't fit prooooooooperly,' she grunted, her eyes rolling in agony.

The Super Moshis grimaced.

'I'll tell yooooou what,' Frau BrownKau said suddenly. 'I'll let you stay for freeeeee – if you locate my false teeeeeth.'

'You're on,' agreed Poppet quickly before the moody cow could change her mind. 'Come on, Super Moshis, let's play "find the falsies"!'

The Super Moshis left the cool, shaded hotel lobby and stepped into the bright, sunny pool area.

The sparkling pool was huge. Its perimeter was dotted with big spa rooms where the gooperstar guests received their treatments.

'This certainly beats swimming at DJ Quack's A-Quack-tic Centre on Taki Taki Island,' said Luvli as she surveyed the celebrities relaxing on their sun loungers. 'Hmph! I see Simon Growl's here.'

'Oh, and there's Zack Binspin!' Poppet squealed. 'Let go over and say hi.'

'First things first, Poppet,' said Katsuma. 'We've got to find Frau Now BrownKau's teeth.'

'First things first nothing! I'm starving! I've got to have something to eat and drink!' Furi cried, his stomach grumbling loudly as he snatched up the hotel menu from a nearby table.

'We can't possibly afford the prices at the Sandy Drain Hotel,' said Poppet, looking over Furi's shoulder at the menu. 'Crispy Bat Wings, 120 Rox! Bongo Colada 78 Rox! It's daylight robbery!'

'It's celebrity snobbery, that's what it is!' Zommer said, outraged. 'But at least the water's free. Here, Furi, wrap your furry gob round this,' he added, handing Furi a half-drunk glass someone had left beside a sun lounger.

'Cheers, Zom,' said Furi. He was about to take a sip when he spotted something at the bottom of the glass.

'Arrrrgh! *Wassat?*'

The Super Moshis bashed heads as they all tried to take a look.

'It's Frau Now BrownKau's missing teeth!' laughed Diavlo, fishing them out.

'I must have left them by the pooooooool when I went to give a treatment in one of the spa rooooooooms,' said Frau BrownKau as she snatched her false teeth from Furi's grubby hand.

Frau BrownKau spat the problem choppers on to the carpet, popped in her own and strode out to the pool area without another word.

The Moshis all looked at the discarded teeth. Suddenly, they sprouted legs and began dashing about madly, gnashing and chattering away!

'Oh my, it's a Jabbering Jibberling!' Luvli exclaimed. 'The poor thing's been stuck in that old cow's mouth the whole time!'

'How cruel!' said Poppet, and bent over to speak to the little Moshling. 'Are you OK?'

'Ewwww-it-smelled-like-grass-in-there-but-I'm-OK-thanks-to-you!!' the Jabbering Jibberling chittered. 'My-name's-Rofl!-What's-yours?'

Poppet opened her mouth to answer but Rofl chattered on.

'I'd-get-out-of-here-if-I-was-you. Don't-trust-Frau-BrownKau! She-does-strange-things.'

'We can't. We're on a mission,' explained Diavlo. 'In fact, we're looking for a Zoshling – have you seen one around here?'

'A-what-ling?' Rofl asked, hopping from foot to foot. 'I-don't-know-what-that-is-but-i-can-tell-you-that-Frau-BrownKau-keeps-a-strange-pet-in-spa-room-three!'